My Dancing Shoes

by Claire Daniel
illustrated by Siri Weber Feeney

Harcourt
SCHOOL PUBLISHERS

Printed in China

ISBN 13: 978-0-15-351548-4
ISBN 10: 0-15-351548-1

Ordering Options
ISBN 13: 978-0-15-351215-5 (Grade 5 Advanced Collection)
ISBN 10: 0-15-351215-6 (Grade 5 Advanced Collection)
ISBN 13: 978-0-15-358138-0 (package of 5)
ISBN 10: 0-15-358138-7 (package of 5)

11 12 13 14 15 0940 12 11 10

My dancing shoes have always had a mind of their own. They never seem to want to go in the direction that I aim them.

I started studying ballet when I was six, and I tried very hard. The only problem was that my shoes were pretty klutzy. When I wanted to go to the right, my shoes grudgingly headed that way only after first pulling me to the left. Sometimes they invented their own steps and threw me off balance.

I almost gave up dancing after my first big recital because my shoes were awful! That was also the day that Hannah became my dreaded enemy. Hannah is one year older than me and is a very talented dancer.

In that particular performance, Hannah had a small solo part with us beginners dancing behind her. I desperately wanted to be brilliant, but my shoes had other ideas and tripped me! If that wasn't bad enough, I bumped into the girl dancing next to me, and she fell. Before I knew it, all six of us were down on the wooden floor! Hannah went on with her solo as planned, but no one noticed, since the rest of us were falling like dominoes around her.

For the next four years, Hannah barely spoke to me. If she did, it was only with a grunt. One time I was sure that she actually sneered at me. I didn't blame Hannah for still feeling angry, but I hoped one day she would forgive me. After all, I was just a little kid when it happened—and I'm not responsible for my shoes!

Now I've gotten new shoes. I've worked very hard since that first recital to learn how to control my footwear. Somehow, they have learned to obey my wishes—usually—and they've transformed me into a decent dancer.

About a year ago, after my baby sister, Gisela, mastered the art of walking, I began teaching her some basic dance steps. If she winds up with the same kinds of shoes I had, she'll need all the time and practice she can get!

Hannah and I were in different dance classes, and we went to different grammar schools, so we rarely saw one another. Last year, though, I got in line for the water fountain after dance class and suddenly found myself standing behind Hannah. I had seen her dance that day and decided to take a chance speaking to her. If I complimented her, she might act more friendly towards me.

I tapped her on the shoulder and said, "You danced well today."

Without looking at me, Hannah walked forward and said, "I need water." My face turned beet red, and I wanted to melt into the floor. She was still angry with me! For the next year, I did my best to avoid her.

When I turned eleven, my mom encouraged me to take a jazz dancing class instead of ballet. Surprisingly, my new dancing shoes seemed to enjoy jazz movement. They followed my instructions much better than my old ballet shoes did.

When I went to my first jazz class, I was in for a surprise. Hannah was in my class! I could tell she was still angry with me from the scowl on her face.

"Hey, Hannah, smile big and look happy!" our jazz instructor always said when Hannah looked my way.

I had come a long way since my first ballet class. Now I danced four times a week, and my shoes were quite well-behaved. Still, a voice inside me said I was not good enough to be in the same class with the talented Hannah.

Late in March, dancers were being chosen for parts in the annual spring performance. At the end of auditions, the instructors said, "Hannah and Jennie will be dancing a duet."

Were my shoes as shocked as I was? The piece we were to perform required two dancers—one who would dance seriously in an old-fashioned style, and one who would mimic her. It was supposed to be a humorous scene.

"Hannah, we want you to be the comic," our teacher said.

"I'm not doing it!" Hannah said indignantly. She stamped out of the room, and Mr. Anston followed after her.

I looked at my instructor Ms. Simms and said, "Why is Hannah doing the comic part? She's a better dancer than I am. Maybe I would be funnier—and this time I would be trying to get laughs."

Ms. Simms said, "Hannah is a good dancer, and so are you, Jennie. That's why we want the two of you to do the number together."

"Hannah doesn't like me very much," I told her.

Ms. Simms said, "Oh, Jennie, I'm sure that's not true." I guess she didn't know our history.

When Hannah and I had a minute alone, I said, "Hannah, I'm sorry about ruining your recital five years ago. I was only a kid then, and I didn't know what I was doing."

"What are you talking about?" she asked, confused.

I said, "Don't you remember when I came onstage during my first recital, and my shoes tripped everyone?"

For the first time, I saw Hannah laugh, and she actually smiled at me. "That was you, Jennie? I had forgotten all about that!"

I said, "I thought you were mad at me all these years."

She smiled again and said, "Well, that's ridiculous because I haven't been. I guess you've seen me when I've been scowling, right? That happens when I get impatient with myself and think I should be doing better. Yeah, I get frustrated with myself a lot."

"Why don't you want to do this dance with me?" I asked.

She said, "It has nothing to do with you. I was just disappointed that I didn't have a solo part. Never mind me—we'll be brilliant together."

For the next month, Hannah and I worked hard on our piece. Sometimes Ms. Simms and Mr. Anston had us switch parts to help us learn how to work as a team. My shoes and I took great pleasure in dancing the comic part, much more than performing the serious one.

Four days before the performance, our costumes arrived. I stuffed my new serious dancer's outfit in my gym bag so that my family wouldn't see it. I wanted to surprise my parents on the day of the show, so when I got home, I carefully hid it in my closet.

The morning of dress rehearsal, I took the new costume out of my bag and held it up to the light, just to admire it. I gasped, horrified at the sight. My formerly white outfit was now covered with bright red smears. I threw it down and searched frantically for my dancing shoes. Did they do the damage?

Urgently, I grabbed the shoes and held them up. They each had a pair of smiling red lips on the toe!

I wanted to scream, but instead I sat down to calm myself. Then I showed my costume to my mom. "It looks like somebody has drawn all over these things with crayons, or markers, or maybe even lipstick," she said. " I'm sorry." She said she might be able to remove the smears, but she couldn't do it that morning because she was late for work.

Sighing, I tucked my costume into my gym bag and left it on my bed while I ran into the kitchen and ate a quick, nervous breakfast.

When I went back into my room, who would have done such a thing became clear. Gisela had my costume, and she was clutching one of my mother's lipsticks! She looked up at me and proudly held up my smirking shoes. I tried to yell at her, but how could I? She didn't know that she had ruined my outfit.

I carefully pried the lipstick from Gisela's hand and took her to my dad in the kitchen. If I hadn't known any better, I would have thought that my shoes were involved in the mischief. They just grinned and grinned.

Before changing into my costume at the dress rehearsal, I pulled Hannah and Ms. Simms aside. Hannah was wearing a plain white leotard instead of her funny outfit.

"My little sister drew all over my shoes and costume with lipstick," I said. "The costume is ruined."

"I think your costume might not be as ruined as you think," Ms. Simms smiled. "We've decided that you should do the comic role. Your red-streaked costume will be perfect for the role and so will you!"

I guess my shoes had the last laugh after all!

Think Critically

1. Why does Jennie think that Hannah doesn't like her?

2. Based on the story and what you know about people, why do you think Hannah snubbed Jennie and didn't speak to her?

3. What advice do you think Jennie would give to her sister when she goes to dancing school?

4. What lesson did Jennie learn in the story?

5. Would you want Jennie to be your older sister? Why or why not?

Music

Ballet Chart Do some research about famous ballets. Find out who wrote each ballet, when it was written, and whether the music is classical or modern. Make a chart with your information. If possible, listen to some of the music.

School-Home Connection Make a list of things you have learned from other family members. Then have your family members add to the list by listing things they have learned from you and other family members.

Word Count: 1,448